LOVED

THE BAD BOY NEXT DOOR - BILLIONAIRE'S PASSION BOOK 3

ALIZEH VALENTINE

HOT AND STEAMY ROMANCE

CONTENTS

Sign Up to Receive Free Books   v
Blurb   vii

1. Chapter One   1
2. Chapter two   6
3. Chapter Three   14
4. Chapter Four   19
5. Chapter Five   23
6. Chapter six   32
7. Chapter Seven   36
8. Chapter Eight   40
9. Chapter Nine   46

Sign Up to Receive Free Books   51
Preview of The Widow's First Kiss   53
Chapter 1   56
Chapter 2   62
Chapter 3   70

Other Books By This Author   81

Made in "The United States" by:

Alizeh Valentine

© Copyright 2020 – Alizeh Valentine

ISBN: : 978-1-64808-118-7

ALL RIGHTS RESERVED. No part of this publication may be reproduced or transmitted in any form whatsoever, electronic, or mechanical, including photocopying, recording, or by any informational storage or retrieval system without express written, dated and signed permission from the author

❀ Created with Vellum

SIGN UP TO RECEIVE FREE BOOKS

Sign Up to Receive Free E-Books and Audiobook Codes.

Would you like to read **The Unexpected Nanny, Dirty Little Virgin** and **other romance books** for **free**?

You can sign up to receive these free e-books and audiobooks by typing this link into your browser:

https://www.steamyromance.info/free-books-and-audiobooks-hot-and-steamy/

Or this one:

https://www.steamyromance.info/the-unexpected-nanny-free/

Nate

One minute you're having a great time living the playboy lifestyle, and the next an ex has a tragic accident and leaves you with a 10-month-old kid! My new daughter Emma is cute as a button, but I'm man enough to admit that I'm overwhelmed. Help appears in the form of the angel next door, Shannon Becker, and though she's confident in her maternal instincts, she seems to have no idea just how drop-dead gorgeous she really is. I never knew that my type would be cute, pear-shaped, and a whiz with kids, but here it is. And before we go much farther, I'm going to make Shannon mine.
Hope she knows that ...

Shannon

My sisters ran off with their hunks, and I was left in my dead grandma's house, trying to make all the decisions while appeasing everyone. When the hot playboy who owns the house next door shows up with a sad baby in his hands, everything changes, and for once, I'm the one taking charge.
Nate Waters is helpless around kids, but I'll show him how to handle things ... and if I'm lucky, maybe that means he'll teach me a few things as well.
I might be the plainest of the Becker sisters, but that doesn't mean that I'm ignorant about what those hot looks of his mean. Nate's the most gorgeous man I've ever met, so it's impossible he's into me ... right?
Both Nate and I have a lot to learn, and it looks like we'll be doing some of that learning together—and in bed!

CHAPTER ONE

Shannon

"So ... you're in Berlin?" I couldn't keep the squeak out of my voice, and Mara laughed at my shock. If I didn't know her better, I would have said that she was drunk—but she didn't need alcohol to sound like that, not when Cade was involved.

"Oh my God, Shannon, it's amazing," she exclaimed. "It's frigid out here, and you can tell there's just so much history rooted in the rock ... And there's this beautiful glow ..."

I could almost picture my glamorous older sister shaking her head as she reined herself in. In the background, I heard Cade speak up, and she said something to him before turning back to the phone and our conversation.

"Listen, Shannon, I've got to go. Are you doing all right?"

"Of course I am," I said a little too sharply. "I'm not going to wither and die because you ran off with your fiancé."

Cade hadn't been her fiancé forty-eight hours ago. Both

Mara and I had thought they were done for good. Somehow he had turned things around, and on Christmas day, had whisked my sister off to Berlin.

"Well, we were planning to spend Christmas day together ... your presents are on the counter."

"Yes, I got the gift certificates," I said dryly. "Thank you. I'll mail yours."

"Well, I might not be heading back to Atlanta for a while," Mara admitted, and I felt my head ache. How in the world did my sisters handle these whirlwind affairs? It all left me dizzy.

"Don't worry about it. Go off and see Berlin. Tell Cade he'd better treat you right."

"Thanks, Shannon." Mara paused. "You're a good sister, Shannon. Don't be too lonely today, okay?"

"That's a silly thing to say," I told her. "Have a good time. Don't get into any trouble."

I heard her laugh at something Cade said as she ended the call. No matter what else I might think of Cade and their relationship, I wasn't sure that I had ever heard my sister laugh like that, and a part of me grudgingly conceded that he might actually be good for Mara.

I wondered if I should call Chloe and tell her about Mara running off to Berlin with a brand-new fiancé, but then it occurred to me that Chloe was probably dealing with a brand-new fiancé of her own the morning after Christmas.

No one had thought it was a good idea for Chloe to get involved with Alex Reed, son of one of the richest, most powerful families in town, but no one could ever tell my baby sister what to do. And it was a good thing, because she and Alex had somehow beaten the odds (and according to some local gossip, had managed to royally piss off the esteemed Reed family in the bargain). They were holed up in Chloe's little apartment in Illinois, plotting their next move.

All of which left me in our deceased grandmother's house in White Pines, still without a clue as to what to do with the place.

"Sorry, Grandma," I murmured to the room at large. "I thought we would have this figured out by now."

Grandma Rose would have just rolled her eyes at us. She loved us all, but she had always been a pragmatic, no-nonsense type of woman. We had spent every Christmas and most summers in White Pines, running in and out of the house under her watchful eye. She loved us, but she gave us our space. We all loved her for that.

She had died a few years ago, and after the house made its way through probate, it had turned out that it was willed to my sisters and me. The question of what to do with the house was what had brought us back to sleepy little White Pines, Wisconsin, this Christmas, but the question seemed just as confusing now as it had been at the beginning of the season.

Was I a little bitter because both of my sisters had somehow fallen in love and run off with their men? Maybe just a little. Chloe was the baby of the family, all big eyes and sweetness, and Mara was the go-getter, with a hot editing gig in Atlanta and charisma to burn.

I was just ... Shannon—with dull brown hair compared to the raven black of my sisters, and gray eyes like Grandma Rose had before me. I also shared with Grandma Rose's side of the family a predisposition to be, shall we say, a little small on top and round on the bottom, to put it politely. Most of the time, I was not too concerned about looking like the innkeeper's wife in a fantasy novel while my sisters looked like the beautiful princess and the icy queen, respectively, but sometimes it did sting.

I sighed, scuffing my worn slippers on the hardwood floor. The house had already waited a few years for a decision, and I supposed it could wait a little longer. I could stay for another week or so, get it shut up properly against the winter, and then it would be back down to Indiana for me, back to the job hunting. My last temp gig had ended with the end of the company, and now that Christmas was over, I didn't have any excuse not to get back into the job search.

I knew that I couldn't afford to stay in White Pines much longer. Not only did I have to think about my dwindling bank, but there was also the fact that a part of me wanted nothing more than to stay. This house held a lot of Becker family history, and the idea of it going on the market—going to some other family—made me ache. However, I didn't have the money to keep it, and neither of my sisters was particularly attached.

This place could be a trap if I let it—though I might not be as sharp as my sisters, I knew that much at least. It was time to get a move on. Sometime after the New Year, I'd call my sisters and make them nail down a decision. Perhaps it wouldn't be as difficult if we weren't surrounded by the memories of our teenage years.

I looked around the house regretfully. I hadn't been so silly as to drag out the tree, but I couldn't resist throwing some of Grandma Rose's artificial pine bough garlands on the mantle place and setting out some candles. My sisters' few presents were arranged prettily on the hearth, but now I wondered whether I should have bothered at all. The effect the day after Christmas was more melancholy than anything else.

Despite knowing that I should be cleaning, planning, and starting the preparations for heading back to Indiana, I couldn't let go of the place just yet. It would feel too much like saying goodbye.

I felt silly and defiant all at once as I pulled up a Christmas mix on my phone and made some cookies from a roll of frozen dough. It was just fine, I told myself. I was getting rid of leftover ingredients and lifting my own spirits a little bit in the process.

As the smell of baking cookies filled the house, I did feel a little better, and I thought maybe I could start figuring out what came next.

However, before I could do anything more than reach for my notebook to start making a to-do list, there was a knock on the front door.

Looking through the peephole, I was startled to see a desperate-looking man in a black coat, with stubble on his jaw and a rather wild look in his eyes, standing on the porch. For a second, I wondered whether I should call the cops, or risk it by opening the door to see if he was in some kind of trouble.

Then his arm shifted, and I could see that he was cradling a baby in one arm. A baby ... wrapped in a towel?

Before I could think twice, I opened the door.

CHAPTER TWO

Nate

Okay, I'll admit it. When I stumbled over the property line to my neighbor's place the morning after Christmas, I probably wasn't thinking straight. I mean, shit, who would be? I'd gotten around four hours of sleep in the last forty-eight, and given the fact that I hadn't actually sold Emma to Santa Claus on the second night she refused to sleep, I thought I was doing pretty well.

When I went to the emergency room after that second night, they told me to go the hell home and take care of my baby—she wasn't dying, and that was a comfort at least. But with just the two of us alone in the little house my mom and dad owned when they were first married, comfort was pretty scarce on the ground.

"God, please be quiet," I groaned, hours after our return from the hospital. "Are you old enough to bribe yet? What the hell can I buy you to make you sleep? Do you like jewelry yet? Boats, cars? What?" Unfortunately, ten-month old babies didn't understand bargaining.

I saw the sunrise the day after Christmas through bloodshot eyes, and at some point, I guess I saw the lady who lived next door shuffling through her kitchen in the morning. Who she was and what she was doing didn't make a difference. What mattered to me at that point was that she looked like she might have gotten more sleep than I had, and maybe, just maybe, she could figure out a solution to the mystery of Emma's terrible crying. I grabbed the diaper bag that had come with Emma, which the lawyer had promised had all the basics, and I was on the porch next door before I could think twice.

When the woman opened the door, I had a brief impression of a pretty face, generous hips, and gleaming brown hair—and then I thrust Emma at her like some kind of wiggling, crying fruitcake.

"Please help," I said, and that was when I realized exactly how fucking insane I sounded.

Instead of calling the cops, though, a look of understanding came over her face, and she took Emma from my arms as if lunatics threw crying newborns at her every day.

"Come in," she said. "It's freezing outside, and that can't be helping."

Some paternal part of me that was suffocating under a lack of sleep had just realized that I'd given my daughter to a stranger, so I followed her closely as she walked back into the kitchen. There was a tiny, guilty part of me that wondered if Emma might be better off if I just ... ducked out of the house and drove hell for leather back to Chicago and points unknown, but the rest of me roared against it. Emma was my daughter—mine —and the fact that I didn't know how to take care of her was shaping up to be the most shameful thing I've ever had to confront in my life.

"They said at the ER that she was fine, that she just had a cold, but she won't stop crying ..."

"I'll bet she does, poor little thing," the woman said absently. All of her attention was on Emma, who was wrapped in a towel because I was afraid that dressing her would make her even more uncomfortable. In the kitchen, under a stronger light, the woman gave Emma a quick examination, moving with a competence that I could only envy.

"Well, there are a lot of reasons babies cry," she said, almost talking to herself. "Has she passed gas or relieved herself this morning? Has she had food?"

"I was at the ER this morning, and I know they cleaned her. She doesn't want any food ..."

The woman passed a hand over Emma's forehead with a frown. "And no real fever, either ...Wait, I know ..."

She tipped Emma up, peeking up my daughter's snub little nose, and for some reason that made her grin. "Ah, got it. Her nose is all mucked up. Let's take care of that, okay, baby?"

Emma kept crying, which didn't surprise me at all, but I blinked when the woman handed the naked baby back to me.

"Um ..."

"This is gonna look kinda bad, but just keep her arms down so she doesn't push me away, okay? I'm going to clean her nose. I think the pressure and reduced air flow is what's giving her so much trouble."

"Do ... Do I get a tissue?"

"Kind of!"

My neighbor looked altogether too chipper about this. She reached into a nearby drawer and pulled out what looked like a blue bulb with a long siphon at one end, rinsing it in the sink before turning back to Emma and me.

"Wait, do you know what you're doing?"

"Yes, I do. Do you want to do this yourself? I can tell you what to do ..."

"No. God, no."

She rolled her eyes at me, which made me feel more than a little ashamed of myself.

"Okay. Then hold her arms, please."

"It's okay, kiddo," I murmured automatically to Emma, and then the woman stuck the siphon into her nose. She worked fast, hitting both of Emma's tiny nostrils before Emma could even start to struggle. As she squirted the disgusting mess onto a tissue she had ready, Emma uttered a sharp cry of surprise, and then miraculously, she stopped crying.

"Oh my God, you're magic," I whispered, and she shot me a worried look.

"Um, not really. Let's see how the baby's doing now ..."

Apparently, having a stuffed nose for two days could really do a number on you. Emma whimpered sharply, and then collapsed in my arms. I was alarmed until a surprisingly loud snore came from her, and then I felt so relieved my spine turned to jelly.

"Good," the woman said with satisfaction. "Just hold onto her for a minute. I need to get the cookies out."

Cookies? I watched in brief confusion as the woman turned around like some kind of domestic goddess, slipping on a plaid oven mitt to whip out two pans of chocolate chip cookies from the oven. I suddenly realized that the air was perfumed with the smell of baking and there were Christmas carols playing, and I felt so out of place that I wanted to stand up and escape before I invaded any more of her space.

"I should probably get on my way," I said awkwardly. "Thank you so much ..."

"Just have a seat," she said, her voice gentle. "You look like you're going to collapse any minute, and if you take her into the cold right now, she'll probably wake up again."

She laughed at my mostly-serious shudder, and it occurred to me that she had a really nice laugh. I did as she said, sitting at the homey kitchen table as she plated up a pair of cookies for me as well as an honest-to-God glass of cold milk.

"When was the last time you ate?" she asked, and I blinked.

"Um. I think I had a doughnut yesterday morning?"

"Okay, two plates of bacon and eggs, coming up. No objections?"

I should probably have objected after already having ruined her morning and making her ... siphon ... my disgusting offspring's mucous, but I had absolutely nothing left. Instead, I nodded and simply sat at her kitchen table, my daughter wrapped again in her towel against my chest.

I blinked awake when a heavy plate piled high with food was set in front of me. I had dozed off without even realizing it and Emma was still fast asleep in my arms.

"Here, you can put her down in this while you eat."

While I was out, she had set up a dresser drawer and lined it with blankets, setting it on the table. If I were a different man, or in a different state of mind, I might have told her that I was worth more than a billion dollars and that my daughter deserved better than sleeping in a drawer, but hell. At that point, if she had pulled out one large enough for me, I might have crawled in too. I set Emma into the drawer carefully and covered her with a towel before sitting down.

We ate in silence at first, and I couldn't stop myself from groaning a bit at how good everything tasted. I'd eaten food from all over the world, prepared by some of the most highly-regarded chefs, but I wasn't sure that anything compared to that meal.

"God, thank you so much," I mumbled when I had taken the first edge off of my hunger. "I don't even know your name ..."

"It's Shannon. Shannon Becker," she said. "And you are?"

"Nate Waters. And the little bundle of joy over there is Emma. We're, uh ... new to each other."

She blinked slowly at me, raising an eyebrow. If I were in LA or New York, any person hearing a statement like that would have been all over me for the details. My folks had always said that Wisconsin was a little more 'mind your own business' than other parts of the country, and apparently this was what they'd meant.

For some reason, the fact that Shannon didn't push me made me want to tell her. Hell, it was a weird story; I barely understood it yet, and I was living it.

"A week ago, I was in the Bahamas, getting away from the ice and snow, doing some windsurfing—the usual."

"Of course, the usual," she said with a wry grin, and I blushed a little before continuing.

"I was set to 'do not disturb' for just about everything, but my lawyer called, which told me that things had definitely gone wrong. I was thinking some kind of corporate espionage, embezzlement—something—so I was on the plane as soon as he had the details for me on the flight to Chicago.

"Turns out an ex from about two years ago, Mandy was her name, had a baby she never told me about. We had a good time, and I thought we'd ended it kind of fast, but that's what happens, right? Things ended; we moved on. Only Mandy ended it fast because she figured out she was pregnant, and she ran off to some hippie granola retreat in goddamn Sweden to have the baby, and I might never have known that Emma existed at all if she hadn't put me on the birth certificate."

"What happened to Mandy?" asked Shannon, and somehow, I could tell that she was already feeling a kind of sympathy for this woman she had never met. The compassion was clear in her eyes, and it made me feel oddly ashamed of myself.

"Mandy got into an auto accident. Nasty and unfortunate, but there it is. And now there's Emma, her daughter and mine, and ..."

I shrugged.

"Mandy and I didn't talk much; our relationship was more about ..." I stopped myself, realizing poor Shannon didn't need to hear *all* my dirty laundry. "Anyway, just about the only thing I knew about her past was that her parents were not great people. They'd sent for Emma in Chicago, and they planned to take her. I ... I couldn't let that happen.

"There was a fight, but having a lot of money and a scary lawyer can really help a lot of things move faster. I have custody now, but after that chaos, I just wanted to get away from everything."

"So you came to White Pines?"

"Yeah. Never been before, but the house next door belonged to my parents. They're gone now, but I never sold the place, and it was an easy enough drive up from Chicago."

"God, that's some story. Poor sweetie."

For a second I thought she had called me 'sweetie' and I was equal parts pleased and confused, but then I realized she was looking at Emma, who was still snoring away in her drawer. Shannon reached over and stroked Emma's flushed cheek, shaking her head.

"Yeah. I ... I need to figure out a lot."

"I can imagine," Shannon said. "I mean, single guy like you, living your life, and you get a kid out of the blue. Learning all the skills from scratch while under fire can't be easy ..."

"Well, by 'figure things out' I meant I was planning on hiring a nanny to take care of all that," I said, and she gave me a look of shock and surprise. Once again I felt that weird sense of shame, something I hadn't felt in a very long time, no matter what my exes thought I should feel.

"Really? Can't you spend some time getting to know her a little? You haven't had a lot of time to bond or anything, and this is an important time period for you and Emma ..."

"I'll admit that I haven't thought about ... bonding or anything like that. It's all happened so fast. But there won't be any bonding happening if she cries herself to death because I don't know how to irrigate her nose, or if I die from lack of sleep because she won't stop crying."

"I guess that makes sense," Shannon said reluctantly. "It just seems sad to me, that's all."

I felt her pulling back a little even though she made no physical move at all. She was reminding herself that I was a stranger and that she really didn't have any business commenting on what I did. I would have said that I was grateful for that, but I wasn't. Instead, I felt strangely alarmed by the idea that she was pulling back at all.

That was when I realized the perfect solution.

"So ... any chance you're looking for a job?"

CHAPTER THREE

Shannon

I stared at Nate, and if I hadn't already met my quota for shock that day by having a desperate man and crying baby appear on my doorstep, I probably wouldn't have known what to say. However, helping Emma breathe again and feeding Nate had made me what my grandmother would have called 'familiar,' and I spoke without thinking.

"Are you joking?" I demanded. "You don't know me from the tree in the front yard. You can't hire me as a nanny."

"Well, I know that you got Emma to sleep, and I know that you make a mean plate of bacon and eggs," he said with a grin. "We can go from there."

In the back of my mind, it occurred to me that a desperate Nate had won instant pity and sympathy from me. A Nate that had gotten a little nap and a full meal inside of him was clear-eyed, almost astonishingly good-looking, and surprisingly convincing. He had a tall, lean build, which I could now see was dressed in expensive clothing, topped with chestnut hair and bright green eyes; I could feel a little flutter in my stomach whenever he fixed his gaze on me like that.

Being a fairly plain girl who wasn't used to much male attention meant that I could be pretty susceptible to handsome men, so I resolved to be careful.

"No, we can't go from there," I argued. "Surely if you're doing as well as you imply, you've got the cash to do a proper search. Find someone with a lot of credentials, interview ..."

He looked around as if I had given him a brilliant idea.

"That's fantastic. Let's get started. How do you know so much about kids?"

I blinked.

"Because I babysat a lot in high school, and I completed two years of pediatric health training before I dropped out of my program."

"Why was that?" he asked, surprisingly concerned, and I shrugged.

"Life, basically. I was doing well, but then I slipped and broke my ankle. That sort of took me out of commission for almost a year, and then I had too much debt to go back. I'm working on paying down the medical debt and getting back to school within the next few years, but ..."

I shrugged again. But it all seemed so far away. The money I owed to the hospital for a simple break seemed insurmountable, and I wasn't sure that pediatric health was even what I wanted to do anymore.

"Well, so it's not like you got kicked out for drugs or seducing the dean or anything."

"No!"

"Good, we're getting somewhere! Do you have kids of your own? Is that why you had that siphon on hand?"

"No, I'm here on my own. I had the siphon because my grandmother used to watch kids from the neighborhood ..."

Somehow, it all came out then. Everything about my Grandma Rose, my sisters and what we needed to do, came tumbling out of my mouth. I thought Nate was going to have some smart remark about it—he didn't seem to be the sort of man who took a lot of things seriously—but instead he watched me carefully.

"You sound like you could use a bit of a break as well," he said, and I frowned.

"Look, no matter how much you love kids, they're work, okay? It's why you need to pay babysitters ..."

"Oh, I know that ... Look, I was taught that spending money is like buying your own time back. Enough money and you have some more choices. What would you say to a job that paid you three thousand a week?"

I blinked because I had never made more than three thousand dollars a month in my life.

"Because that's what I'm willing to give you—three thousand a week to stay here in White Pines and to look after Emma, and maybe to cook me breakfast once in a while. If everything's going well in a month, then a ten-thousand-dollar bonus, too. After that, you can take off, do what you want. But right now, I need someone I trust to look after Emma, and that's you."

I looked at him for a long moment, and something about that seemed to make him uncomfortable. I looked at him a little harder and realized why.

"You don't really trust people easily, do you?" I asked, and he shook his head once.

"No. Not at all, usually. But I can't look after Emma on my own, and I trust you."

I might still have said no, but then I met his eyes. There was something so clear and open about them that I felt as if I could see all the way to the center of him.

"All right," I said with a sigh. "I think that's way more money than you need to spend, but I'll do it for Emma's sake. We can try this out, and hopefully you'll get things figured out."

I suppose there was a part of me that thought even then that if he had some time with the little girl, perhaps he would want to take on more of her care. She was adorable, and the idea of sending her off with a nanny, even one that was competent and well-paid, seemed cold to me.

"Thank you," Nate said, and the warmth in his tone had me looking away. God, had it really been that long since I'd been in relationship? I could feel my attraction to Nate tug at me like a tide. To cover it, I stood up and gathered up the plates.

At least, that's what I'd meant to do. Instead, my hand hit the edge of Nate's dish, and it went clattering to the floor. It was empty and didn't shatter at least, but we both reached for it at the same time. We didn't knock heads together, but it was a close thing, and we were left staring at each other with only a few inches separating our noses. He was bent over in his chair, I was in an awkward half-crouch with one hand balanced on the table, and for some unknown reason he chose that very moment to kiss me.

The first touch of his lips to mine sent a deep shiver through me. It wasn't a heavy or forceful thing; it was incredibly gentle and sweet. He might have started it, but I was the one who deepened the kiss, leaning up so that we could taste each other more soundly.

His mouth was warm and firm on mine, and when he ran the very tip of his tongue along my lower lip, I whimpered. Almost shyly, I allowed his tongue to enter my mouth, and I felt oddly lost to the sensations. He tasted of bacon, of course, but there was something else too. It was simply him, and this close, I could tell he hadn't showered in a bit—but that somehow didn't bother me.

The best way I could describe it was that there was just

something that felt right about kissing him, something bizarrely perfect about holding him so close on the kitchen floor.

At some point, his hands came down on my shoulders, and when his fingers brushed against the sensitive skin of my neck, I whimpered out loud. That was enough to wake me up and send me scrambling back. A more graceful woman would have moved back and gotten to her feet. Me being me, I landed on my rear.

I looked up at Nate with wide eyes, and he looked back at me, equally shocked. I blushed as I imagined what he was thinking. He was a billionaire, or so he'd said, who could probably get beautiful women with a crook of his finger—with his movie star good looks he'd probably have gotten plenty of attention no matter how much money he had.

"We ... we probably shouldn't ..." I started, and then I was never happier for a baby to start crying. Emma had woken up and was whimpering a little. Feeling relieved, I stood and scooped her into my arms.

Then it was time to figure out what Nate had in that ridiculously expensive diaper bag he had brought along. Then I could at least pretend to put the kiss out of my mind.

4

CHAPTER FOUR

Nate

The kiss completely blindsided me. I was usually good at reading the room, and I could always tell when a woman was into me. At best, Shannon seemed confused about me when she wasn't feeling pity or disappointed in me. Plus, not to split hairs, but she was hardly my type. Of course, she was adorable, but adorable really didn't fly in the circles I traveled in, where gorgeous was just a thing you start to take for granted.

Of course, I was willing to bet that no one from the circles I traveled in could have whipped up breakfast the way that Shannon did, or helped me with a baby the way that she had.

I might have done any number of things while Shannon got Emma fed and diapered and rocked a bit, but instead I sat at the table, unable to take my eyes off of this woman. She was focused on my daughter as if Emma were hers, and I had a feeling it had nothing to do with the money I had offered her.

Instead, she dressed Emma warmly and set her down in the living room to play. She even found a few antique-looking toys for Emma to play with, and for what felt like the first time, I watched Emma play calmly and happily, babbling to herself as she did so. Even as Shannon was going through the diaper bag, I could tell she was keeping one ear and one eye on Emma at all times, and that made something in my chest tighten.

"Hmm, is this the baby food you've been giving her? This isn't what I would feed her ..."

I shrugged. "It's what was in there. I was planning on having some more delivered."

Shannon thought about it for a moment.

"Honestly, if you're paying me so much, why not give her the royal treatment? I can make her food myself. She might like that better, and it would be better for her ..."

At this point, I wasn't going to argue with a single thing that Shannon said about what was good for Emma, and as I watched her take some notes in her adorably antiquated notebook, my thoughts drifted back to the kiss. I was becoming less surprised that I wanted to do it again.

Later that afternoon, while Shannon and Emma seemed to be rejoicing in block towers that could be built and knocked down again, and I was considering getting some work done, Shannon looked up at me.

"So, where are we going to be sleeping?"

I blinked, because I hadn't thought about that.

"Well, for the last couple of nights Emma and I have been at our place next door. We have some sheets and a crib over there, but it's, um ... pretty desolate."

"Yeah, that place has been shut up since I was a teenager, so I can't imagine it's in ideal shape. Should you stay here? We certainly have the room."

I agreed, because honestly anything sounded better than sleeping in the empty old house. I must have been out of my mind when I decided to make the trek up to White Pines, but right then it seemed like the most brilliant idea I'd ever had—how else would I have found Shannon?

I brought the crib over, but when I started to put it in one of the bedrooms, Shannon shook her head.

"Some people let their babies sleep alone, but that usually doesn't start for a little while. If she's in my room or yours, she can hear someone breathe and be comforted by how close they are."

"Yours," I said instantly. "If she wakes up and cries, you'll know what to do."

Shannon looked a little disappointed by my abdication of responsibility, but it wasn't like she could argue with me. I should have known that the matter wasn't finished, however, when she called me into the bathroom at seven and told me it was time to bathe my daughter.

"It's good for you to know how," she said firmly. "I'll do it from here on out, but if you get into a situation in the future, Emma shouldn't have to be a rolling sticky mess while she waits for you to hire someone to hose her off." She paused. "Don't hose off a baby."

It was a little nerve-wracking bathing a squirming baby girl in the sink, but with Shannon's calm assurance at my elbow, I was able to manage. At any moment, I was afraid I would hurt Emma or do something to scare her, but soon enough, I realized that she was calming down in the warm water, looking at me and the bathroom around her with equal amounts of curiously.

Despite, or perhaps because of, how frantic the week had been, I had never spent any time really looking at my daughter. I took her in as I washed her, and I felt a deep pang in my chest. God, but she was small. She had chestnut hair like me, but her eyes were a deep chocolate brown. Was that the color Mandy's eyes had been? For the first time, I felt ashamed that I didn't know. A surge of nausea went through me as I wondered what

Emma might ask me one day about her biological mother, and how I would have to say that I just didn't remember ...

"Shh, whatever it is, let it go. Emma can tell you're distracted."

I focused first on Shannon's hand on my arm, and then I looked down to see that Emma's sweet little face was screwed up with concern.

"Oh, kiddo, it's all right. I've got you," I told her, and when I leaned down to kiss her damp head, she chortled. Apparently all it took to change her world was a little bit of comfort form me—and maybe for the first time, I felt a deep bond between us. No matter what happened, Emma would always be my daughter. That stunning realization of permanence sent a strange wave of awe coursing through me.

Under Shannon's careful instruction, I dried Emma off, and then dressed her in the warm pajamas that had fortunately been packed in the diaper bag. By the time I settled her down in the crib, she was practically asleep already.

I pulled back to look at her. Shannon had moved the crib next to her bed, and I realized that she could easily reach through the bars to comfort Emma if she woke in the night.

I glanced at Shannon, who was watching us both from the doorway.

"Did you know that I would feel like this?" I asked, and she smiled.

"Maybe."

That night, long after we all should have been asleep, I lay in my bed and wondered at how the world had changed so drastically for me in just a week. Finally, I couldn't resist getting out of my bed and tiptoeing across the hall. The door was open a crack, and I opened it a little more. I listened to Shannon and Emma breathing, and slowly felt a peaceful calm course through my body.

CHAPTER FIVE

Shannon

It was New Year's Eve, and all over the world people were out in their shiniest best, waiting with bated breath for the first morning of the New Year. Even White Pines had organized a party at the town center, something with a pricey entrance fee and drink tickets.

No matter how often or how determinedly friends and family had tried to get me excited about New Year's Eve, it had always struck me as something stressful and dull. That night, I was waiting for the New Year to roll in while wearing a warm and fluffy nightgown, listening to the sweet sound of Nathan putting Emma to bed. From the couch in the living room, I kept a sharp ear tuned for any signs of distress, and I was pleased to hear Nathan chatting softly with his daughter as she babbled nonsense.

"Oh, really?" he commented. "I had no idea. I'll be sure to take that under advisement. You have a good head on your shoulders, Emma Jean Waters, and I know you're going to go far."

It might have been a little weird for a nanny to sit on the couch while the man who employed her got the kid ready for bed, but by that point, neither of us wanted it any other way. There were times when I had sole charge of Emma, when Nate was preoccupied with work calls or talks with his lawyer, but the vast majority of the time, it was a joint effort. It was just as easy as not to give Nate quick lessons on the care and feeding of a ten-month-old, and more to his surprise than mine, he had taken to it like a duck to water. Once he had gotten over the initial shock and the early days of panic, it was clear that Nate really wanted to be a good father to Emma.

I can't deny that I was relieved. Nate was a man who had it all, but I'd never been all that impressed with rich men—even ones as handsome as Nate. They were used to getting their own way, and that usually meant that they had a lot less sympathy for everyone else. Fortunately, Nate seemed devoted to Emma, and that made me relax around him.

Relax ...

Well.

That was one way to put it, at least. There was probably a reason that pictures that Nate showed me of himself where he was closing a big deal or windsurfing in the Bahamas left me a little cold, while seeing him covered in baby food trying to give Emma lunch made something warm flutter in my chest.

It was probably time to admit that I had a full-out crush on my employer, and that every smile he gave me over a grumpy infant was making it worse. Sometimes he would give my arm or shoulder a squeeze while walking by me in the kitchen and that simple gesture would send a rush of sensation through me. I had it bad, and all I could do was hope that I managed to keep it to myself.

As I was musing over this, Nate appeared in the doorway

wearing a faded T-shirt and pajama pants, a triumphant grin on his face.

"Emma's down and out," he said. "Calls for a celebration, I think—she did not want to get into her pajamas."

"Yeah, it's like she thinks that something cool is happening and she'll miss it if she goes to bed," I said with a laugh. "Joke's on her; we're boring adults."

Nate looked like he was going to take exception to that, and then he blinked.

"It's New Year's Eve, isn't it?" he asked, and I nodded. "Christ. This time last year, I was celebrating at the top of the Eiffel Tower."

"Well, White Pines doesn't have an Eiffel Tower, but there's a party going on downtown if you want to go out," I suggested. "I mean, technically, that's what I'm here for, after all."

To my surprise, that made Nate frown. "That hardly seems fair."

"Actually, it's totally fair," I laughed. "You specifically pay me to watch your kid when you can't. Or did you forget about that?"

Nate shook it off brusquely, and I wondered a little bit at that.

"No reason we can't have our own New Year's Eve right here," he said, striding into the kitchen. "Let's see what we've got ..."

I padded into the kitchen after him, curious, and before I knew what he was about, he had pulled some ingredients out of the fridge and started putting together a meal. I usually handled the cooking, and I loved baking. Seeing him cook made me smile, especially when he nodded at Grandma Rose's seasoned cast iron and insisted on preheating the pan.

"Secret to a good steak is to make sure you don't overcook it," Nate murmured. "A nice sear while leaving it pink inside is ideal ..."

He plated the steak and some roasted vegetables in front of us a short time later, and looked around with a slightly wry eye.

"I would say something about how the mighty hath fallen, but God. This is way better than a drafty countdown in Paris where half the people are models and the other half are only there because they want to sleep with the models."

"I don't think it's falling if you're happier about where you are," I commented. "Quite the opposite, really. God, this is good steak ..."

It was delicious, and since it had been a while since lunch, we fell on the food like hungry wolves.

"Did you ever do fun things for New Year's?" Nate asked suddenly. "Am I keeping you from some hot party or some midnight kisses??"

"Oh God, no, you've mistaken me for someone interesting—one of my sisters, maybe. If I'm watching the ball drop, I'm in my pajamas on the couch."

"Not even some champagne?"

"Don't really care for the stuff, I guess ..."

Nate hummed for a moment, and then went to the fridge. He pulled out two juice boxes that we kept as a treat for Emma and I laughed.

"Seriously? You left Paris for all of this ..."

"Shush, Shannon. We're going to take our fine beverages and watch some New Year's television."

And we did. We both ended up on the couch watching celebrations all over the world on Nate's laptop, and as we watched, our bodies drifted closer and closer together. I became aware of it in odd starts and bursts—of how his arm was draped over my shoulders, how nicely I fit against his body. There was something small in the back of my mind telling me that I was playing with fire, but the rest of me only cared about how good it felt.

We finally got to the countdown in our time zone, and Nate

insisted on chanting along, our juice boxes in our hands. It was funny and silly, and I dimly realized I had never loved New Year's Eve as much as I loved it in that moment.

We chanted along with the people on the screen, and I felt a tug of anticipation deep inside. The New Year was on our doorstep, and who knew what it would bring—what new adventures it might have in store for us.

"One!"

On the laptop screen, fireworks went off, people set off noisemakers, broke into the chorus of Auld Lang Syne, and kissed each other passionately in front of the cameras. On a couch in White Pines, Nate and I turned to each other, meeting each other's eyes with a strange tension in the air.

I should have stood up and walked away, but then Nate's arms came around me, drawing me close, and his mouth covered mine. Our first kiss had tasted like bacon. This one tasted like apple juice, but I quickly forgot all about that as I was lost in the torrent of passion.

It was as if I had been waiting for this kiss my entire life, as if we were two parts that had finally found what would make us whole. I gave myself up to the kiss because there was no way I could do otherwise, and when his tongue slid between my lips, I opened to him greedily.

"God but you're beautiful," Nate whispered unsteadily. "Feels like I've been waiting to do this for ages ..."

His mouth moved from mine, and I whimpered at the loss for a moment. Then his lips were traveling along my jawline, then down my neck, tantalizing the sensitive skin there. It made me whimper and groan against him, as I pressed my body closer to his. There was nothing hurried or impatient about the way he moved over me. He moved as if we had all the time in the world, as if all he wanted to do was learn more about how good he could make me feel with his hands, his lips, his breath.

When Nate worked his way to the collar of my nightgown, I blushed a little. Flannel was hardly anyone's fantasy, but Nate ignored my soft muttered protests. He slid his kisses along my collar, and then he reached for the pearl snap buttons that kept the garment closed. With every pop, he bared another few inches of skin. By then I was stretched out flat on my back on the couch, Nate kneeling on the ground beside me.

I felt like some kind of goddess being worshiped, receiving the pleasure that was my due. Nate bared my breasts, lapping gently at the curves while his fingers plucked at the peaks. My breasts had always been sensitive, and he skirted the space between pleasure and over-stimulation with ease. It made me moan and sigh, wanting more of him, but he pulled back a little, tugging another few buttons open.

For a moment, I wanted to cover the rise of my belly and the swell of my hips with my arms. Models, he had said, and I was pretty far from what a model looks like. Instead, Nate brushed away my hands, sliding a loving touch over all of that flesh that had never felt so wonderful and so cherished before. His touch could take me out of my head, and that was exactly what he did. He lavished kisses and caresses over my body until I forgot that I was just Shannon Becker, lying in an old fuzzy nightgown.

I gasped when he brushed his hand over the soft mound below my belly, grazing it first with the back of his hand and then with his fingertips.

"Can I touch you, Shannon?" he asked softly. "I want to so badly ..."

At that point, there was likely nothing in the world that I would have denied him. I shaped the word 'yes' with my mouth, too overcome to get any actual sound out, and Nate smiled. I could see the glint of white teeth in the dimness of the room.

"Perfect, darling. Don't worry. I'm going to take good care of you."

He moved closer to me, stroking between my legs so that they fell open for him. Before he could do much more, however, I reached up to cup my hand over the back of his neck, halting his movement.

"Shannon ...?"

"I want you naked too," I implored, and he smiled, nodding a little.

He stood up to shed his clothes, and then he was magnificently naked in front of me. His body was lean and muscled, beautiful in the way that male bodies can be. His belly was firm with muscle, and below it, his cock jutted out towards me. Eyes half-lidded, I reached for it, stroking the soft skin and swirling my fingers around the head. There was a bead of cloudy liquid there, and Nate stifled a groan when I touched it gently.

"You have no idea what you're doing to me," Nate growled, and I couldn't stop myself from smiling a little.

"I might have some idea," I admitted, and he laughed.

"Wicked girl ..."

I muffled a gasp as he came down over me, his weight pressing me into the couch. Most of his weight rested on his elbows, but it was simply delicious, feeling his full length caging me in from every direction. I could feel his cock pressed against my thigh, feel the differences between our bodies that made such a beautiful contrast.

He slid down so that his cock was pressed between my legs, and as I relished the warmth of him at that intimate juncture, he started kissing me again. Nate dropped kisses all over my face, even my eyelids and the tip of my nose.

I wanted more than kisses now, though. I wanted him, and I wanted everything he had to give me. He shuddered when I ran my sharp nails over his back, burying my face in the crook of his neck.

"I need you now," I said, my voice barely more than a whisper. "Please, Nate ..."

Something about the way I said 'please' made him shiver, and he nodded.

"I wanted to play with you, draw it out—bring you to climax over and over again ..."

"Later," I insisted. "I just ... want you so much ..."

"Greedy little thing," Nate teased, and for a moment I wondered with a sinking heart if he was just going to tease me for a small eternity before giving me—giving both of us—what I wanted.

Then he slid his body over mine, and the same tension that had had me in its thrall seemed to come over him as well.

"God, I can't resist you," he murmured, more to himself than to me.

He slid inside me with a single sure thrust, drawing a cry from my lips. He stopped, looking down at me with concern, but I shook my head.

"Just ... just a second," I whispered, pressing my face against his chest. I wasn't as ready as I had thought, and the slight shiver of pain shocked me.

"Do we need to stop?" Nate asked, his voice steady.

The idea of stopping was far worse than the pain, which was already fading to be replaced with a high note of pleasure.

"No, no, don't stop," I begged, and I spread my legs wider, curving them over his hips.

This small motion seemed to drive Nate wild, and suddenly he was thrusting into me over and over again, pulling out halfway to drive his full length back into me.

The pleasure that I had felt before when he was just touching me was nothing compared to the tumult of pleasure from this, how it rolled over me like the waves of the ocean. Each stroke pushed me higher and higher, and it was almost too much—but not quite. I was brimming with need, every muscle in my body straining for it.

I trembled on the edge, and then with a growl of desperation, Nate grabbed my hips and lifted up to his knees, dragging me with him. The strength and the power of that move, coupled with the new angle, brought a surge of pleasure through me and I jammed my own hand into my mouth as I trembled to completion.

When the waves of pleasure finally receded, I looked up at Nate—who was still thrusting into me. I could tell he was close—so close—and when he thrust into me one last time, I reached up to cover his mouth with my hand as well. I felt the sharp edge of his teeth, but he didn't bite. He remembered that Emma was sleeping not all that far away, and he shook in silence, flooding me with his desire.

Nate collapsed on top of me, and though I knew he would be too heavy soon, for the moment, I relished the pleasure of it.

There might be hell to pay later, but right now, he was all I wanted.

CHAPTER SIX

Nate

When Shannon stirred in my arms, my first instinct was to tighten them around her. The idea that she would leave, just the idea of it, made something in me panic. Then I realized how utterly insane that sounded, so I reluctantly let her go.

"Wow, that was ..." She laughed a little, gesturing aimlessly with her hands as she sat up.

"I'll take anything that doesn't sound like an adjective of amazing as a request to try again immediately and do better," I quipped, but at the worried look in her eyes, I sat up as well.

"What, what's the matter?" I asked. "Is everything all right?"

"It really was amazing," she said with a soft laugh. "Maybe that's part of the problem."

I raised an eyebrow at that.

"I've not often been accused of being *too* good in bed ..."

She shook her head, reaching over to squeeze my hand as if perhaps I was the one that needed comfort.

"What are we doing, Nate?"

"We just had a very good time in bed. What else do we need to be doing?"

Shannon looked up at me with large eyes of such a pure clear gray that I thought I could fall straight into them. There was sorrow there and worry as well. I gave in to my urge to gather her to my chest, and thankfully, she allowed me to do so.

"What's the matter, sweetheart?" I murmured. "Tell me all about it."

"I just ... this isn't something I do lightly," she said. "I know it's not ... it's not popular or fashionable to be hung up on the idea that sex actually means something, but I am. The idea of this meaning nothing ..."

I blinked.

"What makes you think this meant nothing to me?"

"Well, you talked so much about models ..."

All right, maybe I had, and she wasn't wrong when she said that most of those encounters were more about having some fun than anything else. All of the women had treated it the same way as I had, and I supposed that for a long time, that had been fine with me.

For what felt like perhaps the first time, it wasn't fine now.

"This isn't nothing for me," I said firmly. "I don't know what it is, but I wouldn't have done this with you if it meant nothing."

She shot me a skeptical look, and I sighed. "Shannon, you're not that kind of girl."

"No, I'm not," she said, looking down. "I'm shaped like a ridiculous pear; I wear flannel to bed; and my idea of perfume is lotion ..."

"Goddamn, sweetheart, what the hell? No. That's not what I meant at all. You don't do casual, and if I wanted casual, I wouldn't be here."

She looked up at me in surprise.

"What are you saying?" I could see it then, all of the rejection and pain and sadness that she had endured through her life. I could have cheerfully slaughtered every man who ever made her feel as if she wasn't enough, as if she was plain and dowdy, but I realized I could do far better just by telling her what I felt in my heart, what I had been feeling for some time now.

"I didn't expect this to happen tonight, but for a while now, I've felt ... drawn to you. At first I thought it was just seeing how you were with Emma. But that's not it—there's something truly special about you, Shannon, something that draws me in like a moth to fire."

"Nate ..."

"I want you," I said bluntly. "I want you with me. I want to hold you and touch you. I want more than that."

She lowered her eyes, and I thought I could see her feelings warring with her common sense. It wasn't like she was wrong—there were a dozen reasons why this might be a terrible idea. However, I had always been a gambler, and I wanted her—I was willing to bet that she wanted me as well, and I willed her to make the choice that might make us both so very happy.

"I don't know quite what I feel for you yet," she admitted. Shannon, I could tell, would always be a woman who insisted on perfect honesty, and even if it was irritating, it meant that I would always know exactly where I stood with her.

"That's all right."

"But I think I want to find out. If that's all right?"

Something about the shy but defiant way she said those words made me warm to her even more, and I clasped her close to me.

"Perfectly all right. I don't want to push you into something that's wrong for you—or wrong for me, for that matter. I always want you to be happy."

As I said it, I knew it was the truth. At some point, Shannon's happiness had become important to me—a bright glow that I wanted to shield from the troubles of the world.

She cuddled close to me, and I frowned at how cold she was.

"We should probably get to bed," I said with a sigh. Dear God, there was a time when I wouldn't have considered stopping until dawn, but that was apparently in the past. Knowing Emma, she would probably be up and demanding breakfast by seven.

"Will you ... that is ... can I sleep with you?" Shannon asked hopefully, and I felt my heart squeeze again.

"Yes. Absolutely."

For every night of our lives, a small voice in my head said, and instead of frightening me, it made me smile.

CHAPTER SEVEN

Shannon

It only took me a few days into the New Year to figure out that I had lied to Nate. I didn't like lying, and I tried to do it as little as possible, barring the small white lies that keep the world spinning. However, a few mornings after our beautiful night together, as I watched Nate cuddle Emma against his shoulder while looking out over the snowy morning lawn, I realized that I did know how I felt about him.

He caught me looking at him and raised an eyebrow at me. "Do I have yogurt on my face or something?"

"Not at all. You look just fine," I promised, but I came over to run a fingertip over the corner of his mouth anyway. He leaned down to kiss me with Emma sandwiched between us, and I knew the truth.

I loved Nate Waters.

It felt like some kind of ridiculous Cinderella story, but it was true—and it was happening to me. Grandma Rose had always said that it was as easy to love a rich man as a poor man, but that the key to all of it was love. Without love, you might as well be alone, and I suppose for the last few years I had thought I just might be—alone forever.

Now I was in love with Nate Waters, and with every look, every touch, every word, it grew larger and harder to ignore.

Once, I had looked up some news articles about him, the billionaire playboy who owned property on nearly every continent—the golden boy with the golden touch. I had expected not to like Nate's playboy times very much, but I was startled when I found myself pitying him as well. There was something sad and desperate about those interviews, about the man who insisted on showing off his wealth in place of anything that might have been real.

"Is this real?" I asked him one night after we had made love. The master bedroom had been refitted with dark brown embroidered silk sheets and coverlets, turning it into something dim and elegant. It felt like making love in an ancient seraglio, and afterward, I felt oddly unmoored in space and time.

"Of course it is," Nate had responded, cradling me close. "I'm real, you're real, and we can have this for as long as we like."

I believed him. Perhaps it was foolish and heedless, but even though I knew his reputation, I also thought that he was giving me something he had never given to another woman before.

What we had was real.

Every day, we cared for Emma together, and I couldn't deny the fact that I was falling in love with her as well. She was a bright, sassy little girl who was picking up her crawling speed with nearly supernatural ability. She was fearless and curious, and when she accidentally bumped her head or scraped her arm, she made sure we both knew it with bellows of pain and surprise.

The first time Emma hurt herself, Nate had nearly insisted on taking her back to the emergency room. I had to comfort them both as I got a bandage onto Emma's elbow, and then I showed Nate how to kiss it better. That calmed both of them down, and afterward, I laughed at an abashed Nate.

"She's really a lot tougher than you think she is," I promised, but he shook his head.

"I don't have any doubts about how tough she is, but I'm seriously beginning to worry about how tough I'm not. Is it always going to be like this?"

I was a little amused that he was easily five or six years older than I was, but he looked at me as if I had all the answers—at least when it came to Emma.

"Oh, I think it'll probably stop when she hits, say, thirty or so," I said, amused. "You've still got her first day of school, the first time she has a crush, her teenage years, college ..."

Nate shook his head and as Emma crawled away to investigate the fascinating world behind the coffee table, he dragged me in for a quick kiss.

"That all sounds terrifying," Nate confessed. "Just promise me that you'll be around to help cushion the blow. And definitely for kisses afterward."

The hell of it was that I was thinking of it. I'd always been a terrible daydreamer. Where Mara was always off doing exciting things, and Chloe could fall into an adventure by walking to the grocery store, I was the homebody who spent all of her time lost in her thoughts. Now I was having an adventure of my own, and I couldn't stop myself from thinking about what might happen.

I was happy and Nate seemed happy as well. There was a certain calm that seemed to fill him when he held his daughter, when the three of us were together. I dreamed of us seeing the places that Nate talked about so eagerly, and about watching Emma grow.

Though thoughts of far-off places and distant lands were engaging, I found myself startled by the dreams that were closer to home. I suppose it started when I'd caught Nate replacing a board on the rear steps, tamping down fresh wood after replacing the old worn step that had been rotting through.

"It was bothering me," he said with an almost shy shrug, and I thought about what it would be like to actually live at the house in White Pines. It could be our place.

I knew it was all a fantasy. We hadn't known each other a full six weeks yet, but I had simply never felt something so right and so perfect.

I wanted to tell Nate all about my thoughts, but for some reason I held off. We were getting along so well, caring for Emma during the day, making love at night, and learning about each other in the meantime.

I wasn't ready to change things just yet, and as it turned out, I was right to keep my dreams to myself.

CHAPTER EIGHT

Nate

No one was ever ready for things to change. White Pines in the winter was a quiet place, the whole town seemingly wrapped around in a snowy cocoon, and I was happier than I had ever been before. I forgot all about the outside world, all about anything that could ever hurt me or Emma and Shannon.

That Tuesday morning, I was on the phone with some pros I had handling the European properties. I wanted to hear more about what it would take to bring a lot of my business back to the United States, allowing me to stay closer to home. I was thinking about White Pines as home, and that was just fine.

There was a knock on the door, but I didn't think anything of it—it could have been the mail or maybe someone going door to door to collect for some good cause. It was that kind of neighborhood.

I registered Shannon opening the door, and then I heard her voice.

"Nate? This man wants to speak with you."

There was something so odd about her voice that I hung up on the meeting without even thinking about it, coming out to the front room. I didn't know what was going on but I was ready for a fight. Emma was safe in her playpen, and I caught her wide eyes watching me as I strode forward.

The man on the doorstep was a lawyer. After a while, you got to know the look. He was neat, professional, and had no interest in considering anyone in this house as a human being.

"Are you Nathan Waters?" he asked, and for one desperate minute, I wanted to deny it. I knew enough to know that whatever was coming next was going to change everything, and it was almost too much to bear.

"Yes, I am."

He made me sign for a sheaf of official-looking papers, and then he turned around and left. I ignored Shannon's startled questions, taking the papers back into the kitchen. I was distantly aware of her comforting Emma in the living room as I read. It already felt as though they were in another world entirely as Shannon got Emma ready for her nap. I kept reading.

As I read onward, I felt myself sinking into a dark morass of rage and despair, the darkest I'd ever felt. The word *no* shaped itself in my mind over and over again. I didn't realize that I was almost hissing the word through gritted teeth until I caught sight of Shannon's frightened face.

"Nate, what's the matter?"

"Mandy's parents, the scums. They're alleging that my lifestyle is too perverse for a little girl—they're saying that obviously I'm up to no good because I practically stole her from their arms. They're ... stopping just short of accusing me of being a sexual deviant, and somehow they got a goddamn judge to sign off on it, and now I have to defend my custody in court!"

Shannon went pale, her hands flying to her mouth. Her quick glance at the back room reminded me that Emma was down for her nap. I had gotten good at staying quiet while that was happening, but apparently that was all out the window now.

"Surely your lawyers can ..."

"Yes. Probably. Mandy's parents are wealthy enough, but nothing on my level. They're well-respected though, and the judge is probably a friend of theirs. They once shut Mandy up in a closet for four hours because she wouldn't eat her goddamn dinner, and they think I'm unfit?"

Shannon looked as sick as I had felt when my ex had told me about that. There were tears in her eyes, and I felt a pang of guilt.

"God, I'm sorry. Come here ... I'm raving like a goddamn mad man."

She crossed the floor to rest in my arms, and I realized that having her so close gave me as much comfort as I had meant to give her. She held onto me tightly, and we rocked together for a moment. Usually when we were this close, we had romance on our minds, but this was for the pure comfort of having a human nearby who shared our fears and our dreads.

"We'll get through this," Shannon murmured, though it was a tossup whether she was speaking to me or to herself. "I promise, we'll get through this. We're not going to lose Emma, and I swear I will be with you every step of the way."

It took a few minutes for the words to penetrate. The human brain has an amazing capacity to find solutions, and in that moment of stress and fear, I thought I had found one.

"You're going to be here? Every step of the way?"

She blinked at me, hearing the change in my tone.

"Of course, no matter what. I care about Emma, I care about ..."

"Right, right, that's the solution," I said, my mind racing ahead furiously. "They can't call me a damned deviant if I'm married or if I have a house in Wisconsin—if everything looks as if it came out of a postcard ..."

"What are you saying?" gasped Shannon, and I turned to her.

"God, you couldn't be more perfect," I mused. "We'll get married. The hearing's in eight weeks, and we can even backdate the marriage—make it look like some kind of secret romance thing. The press loves that ..."

"You want us to get married?" Shannon exclaimed.

"Yeah. You're the perfect wife and mother, and this is the perfect house. We're going to make this work. No judge in his goddamn right mind will take Emma away from this."

I glanced at her pale face. Shannon looked alarmed, and I realized I was probably moving pretty fast. I grinned at her, that hard steel-edged grin that had scared so many of my competitors straight out of business. She took a step back.

"This is going to be perfect," I told her. "They'll take one look at you and be sold on this. We'll get married, justice of the peace—hell, we can probably send away for it. This sounds like combat pay to me, and it's worth a twenty-thousand-dollar bonus on top of what I'm already going to give you. There's going to be a metric fuck ton of non-disclosure agreements of course, but that's easy enough ..."

"Stop!"

Shannon's voice cracked like a whip. I stuttered to a stop, and in the bedroom Emma started crying frantically. Shannon gave me a vicious glare over her shoulder as she stalked to the bedroom, scooping Emma up in her arms.

My daughter quieted immediately in her arms, and it gave me a quick pang as I saw how very much Emma trusted her.

"Fake marriage? Bribes? Nate, you are being just as devious as they're saying you are. Are you serious?"

I narrowed my eyes at Shannon, crossing my arms over my chest.

"I'm doing what needs to be done, Shannon. This is what I need to do to keep Emma safe."

To my shock, her face crumpled, and tears welled up in her lovely gray eyes.

"I'm not going to marry you for money, Nate," she whispered. "I'm not ... I can't. I won't."

"We need to keep Emma safe," I growled. Emma made a soft distressed sound and patted at the tears on Shannon's face with a soft baby hand. It broke my heart. I wanted to fold them both into a bear hug, but right now, I wasn't sure I had the right.

"Of course we do, and we'll do it the right way. Lawyers, evidence that they were abusive to Mandy, anything we need—everything. I'll sell this damn house myself to pay a lawyer if I have to. But Nate ... There is no way on this planet that I'm going to marry you for some ... some kind of legal scam."

It wasn't a scam, I wanted to say. We were already together—we felt so much for each other. Wasn't this something that she felt as well? Wasn't it something she wanted? I wanted to tear out my hair that she was fixating on something so minor.

"That would be wrong. And what would you tell Emma in the future when she asked you? That her biological mother died, and the woman who loved her like a daughter was ... some kind of actress you hired on for the role? No. Nathan, I can't do that, and I won't let you do that to Emma. Never."

I was stunned by the expression on her face. I had never before looked into a woman's eyes and so clearly seen that her heart was breaking. Plenty of women had told me that their hearts were breaking before, but now I could see that they had been lying or simply had no idea what true grief was. It looked like Shannon was barely holding herself together.

After a long moment of silence, she handed Emma to me

with trembling hands. My daughter whimpered at the exchange, as if she could sense in her baby heart that something was very, very wrong. With a desperate sound, she reached for Shannon. Then she looked up at me as if in confusion, and I didn't know what to tell her.

"I think you had better leave," Shannon said, and she turned away.

CHAPTER NINE

Shannon

Two days later, I got a check in the mail. I thought I was doing pretty well that morning, getting out of bed, dressing in proper clothes and getting myself some food for the first time in who knew how long. Then I found that check, printed out by some cold accountant somewhere, and my whole body shook.

It was for a full twenty thousand dollars, double the bonus he had promised me. The money that Nathan had given me every week had been sitting untouched in my bank account. This was another reminder that our relationship was over, and that if we were being honest with each other, it had never been much of a relationship in the first place. He had forgotten, and I had forgotten for a time, too, but here was the reality of it in front of me.

Pride demanded that I shred the check and never think of Nathan again. Mara would have, and I suspected that after a hard cry, Chloe would have as well. I was always the practical one, however, and I knew what that twenty thousand dollars could do. It meant that I could keep my grandmother's house. I could just live in White Pines for a while, figuring things out.

Mourning.

I was in mourning, and there was no reason to deny it. I felt as if everything in me was withered and dry, as if I might rattle if I moved too quickly. All of the crying had left me feeling strangely light, but not in a comforting way.

I pushed the check back into the envelope and left it on the kitchen table. I didn't want to think about it at the moment. January was such a slow and bitter month, and after everything that had happened with Nate, I didn't think I'd be getting any happier with it.

Nate and Emma had filled the house with a kind of life that reminded me of being a little girl. Grandma Rose had been widowed long before I was born, and she had worked to keep the house full of friends and family. Three young girls who showed up for the holidays helped, and I thought I could understand why she did it now. The place was simply too lonely with just one person—I felt that more clearly now than ever before.

"Did you miss Grandpa as much as I miss Nate?" I asked out loud. "God, I wish I had thought to ask you that."

Despite the check on the table, I virtuously pulled open my laptop to look for local jobs. Without any real conscious decision on my part, it looked like I had decided to stay in White Pines—at least for a while.

I sipped some tea and kept working, because at least if I were working, I wouldn't have to look at the emptiness of the house. I would have to pay attention to the way it seemed prone to echoes and chills now that I was all alone in it.

The sun was just starting to go down when I heard a knock at the door. Belated Christmas delivery? Some charitable organization? Without thinking much about it, I went and opened the door, receiving a shock that was equal parts surprise and déjà vu.

A month ago, I had opened that same door to a desperate man and a crying baby. Now, Nathan was well-dressed and clean shaven, but the desperate look in his eyes was the same. Emma wasn't crying at all, but was bundled up in a warm coat with a pink bobble hat on her head. The moment she set eyes on me, she giggled with delight, reaching for me with one arm.

"Nate! What are you doing here?"

"It's cold. Can I come in?"

There was a kind of urgency to his voice that made me step back. He and Emma came in with a gust of cold air behind them, as if they were carrying winter in their coats. I shut the door behind them, turning to Nate with concern. I couldn't find him for a minute, and then I looked down.

Nate was kneeling on the floor behind me, hand open and out. Instinctively I reached for him, and he took my hand. His face trembled, and for a moment, he simply pressed my hand against his cheek, almost as if he was too shy to kiss it.

"Nate? What are you ..."

"You ... you put up with a lot from me," he began, and I felt a bit of temper spark in my mind.

"Well, I was being paid for it, wasn't I?" I said bitterly. "Thank you for the check. It came today."

Nate actually winced at that, but he didn't let go of my hand.

"God, Shannon, I was wrong. I'm sorry. What I was proposing ... it hurt you, and I didn't even realize how it was going to hurt me too. Not until ... not until I was afraid it was too late. I hope to God it's not, though."

"Nate, what are you saying?"

He looked up at me, and I could have fallen into his eyes forever.

"I did this all wrong before, and right now—no matter what you say—I want to do it right."

My heart started to beat faster, and I didn't know what to think. It was happening so fast, but from the moment I had laid eyes on the two of them standing on my doorstep, my heart had started crying out with need for both of them. I had spent the last little while feeling as empty as a pail, and now that Emma and Nate were here, I felt whole again. The idea that this was more than just a temporary reprieve thrilled me to my core, but at the same time, I drew back, uncertain.

"Nate, we can't ..."

"I love you," he said forcefully. "I love you in ways that I didn't even know that I could love someone. I look for you even when I know that you're not around, and I can't explain to myself, let alone to Emma, why you're not there. I think about you all the time, and it feels like a part of me is missing and there's nothing I can do to fix it."

I felt my chest ache at his confession because that was how I had felt while apart from him as well. He squeezed my hand, looking up at me with those pleading eyes.

"I need you, and I love you, and I think you love me too. I ... I want you to marry me, Shannon. Not as some kind of ploy to get Mandy's parents to back off, not as some kind of ... of power move. I want you to marry me because we fit together. We can stay in White Pines, or I'll take you anywhere in the world—anywhere you like—just stay with me and Emma. Be my wife. Please."

The word was on my lips before he had even finished, and my eyes filled with tears of happiness.

"Yes. Nate, oh yes, yes, I will marry you! I love you."

He rose up to his full height, crushing me to his chest with his free arm. Nestled in his other arm, Emma embraced me as well, knocking her head against my cheek and giggling the whole time.

"I love you," I repeated. "God, I love you so much."

The End

SIGN UP TO RECEIVE FREE BOOKS

Sign Up to Receive Free E-Books and Audiobook Codes.

Would you like to read **The Unexpected Nanny, Dirty Little Virgin** and **other romance books** for **free?**

You can sign up to receive these free e-books and audiobooks by typing this link into your browser:

https://www.steamyromance.info/free-books-and-audiobooks-hot-and-steamy/

Or this one:

https://www.steamyromance.info/the-unexpected-nanny-free/

PREVIEW OF THE WIDOW'S FIRST KISS
A BILLIONAIRE AND A VIRGIN ROMANCE - DREAMS FULFILLED BOOK 1

By Scarlett King

∼

Blurb

The afternoon that the mistletoe sprigs appear all over town, impoverished military widow Lorena Webster is about to spend her last twenty dollars so that her daughter Cindy can at least have one Christmas gift. As they walk down to the toy store from the apartment they share with Lorena's sister Andie, they happen to see Lorena's longtime man crush window shopping up ahead.

James Norris is a heartthrob actor turned billionaire producer who returns upstate every year to visit his family. He's shopping for a replacement gift for his mother, after accidentally leaving her Tiffany lamp at home, when he notices the lovely young mother in the inadequate coat coming his way. Caught under the mistletoe, he's startled and amused when the little girl in her arms leans over and kisses his cheek as she passes by.

Lorena and James quickly connect as the determined Cindy plays Cupid. But there's just one problem: James's meddling ex Andrea Case is using his family Christmas as a bid to get him back—and she has James's gullible mom on her side.

Lorena

All I want for Christmas is to give my little girl any Christmas at all. Since my husband Manny died in Afghanistan in a military operation that couldn't go on his record, I never received any death benefits, or even a body to bury. For two and a half years, we've been living on the edge of starvation while I work two jobs and scramble to save our house. It's been hell—and I've done everything in my power to shield my little girl from the worst of it.

But then comes the day when my baby girl leans over to kiss a random stranger under the mistletoe while I'm walking by. The stranger turns out to be *the* James Norris, a hot Hollywood producer worth more money than anyone could ever spend. And the weirdest part of all is—he's wonderful. And he likes me. When he promises me and my little girl to give us a proper Christmas after all, I wonder if I'm getting a second chance at love—and life.

James

When the prettiest young widow in the world comes walking into my life with her adorable daughter, I fall pretty damn fast. I've put my career first for most of my life, and now that I'm past forty, I'm starting to wonder if it's time to think about all the things I sacrificed. Like having a family. Having a sweet face to wake up to in the morning, and loving arms to fall into at night. Lorena just might be the right person to fix all of that for me.

Winning her over is going to take some work; she has a baby daughter to protect, along with her own broken heart. But that's not the complication I'm worried about. My ex, expert gold digger Andrea Case, is inserting herself into my family's Christmas celebration, manipulating my mother into making sure she can stay. Is she going to ruin Christmas? Or can I find out a way to save it for all of us?

CHAPTER 1

Lorena

Twenty dollars has never made me feel so happy. It's December 23rd and finally, after months of scrambling to keep the heat on and have food in the fridge, I have twenty dollars leftover to buy my baby daughter, Cindy, a Christmas present. It hurts to be this grateful for something so small—especially when Christmas dinner will be a cheap takeout pizza—but it's still a relief, something I haven't felt in months.

So when I walk out of the front door with my two-year-old nestled in my arms, a thick wool blanket wrapped around us both to make up for our inadequate jackets, I'm distracted enough by our good fortune that I don't notice the mistletoe at first.

Phoenicia is one of those tiny little towns in Upstate New York that survives on being pretty, having touristy shops and venues, and having the only late-night gas station for several miles. It has a bed and breakfast, a theater, a fifties-style diner, boutiques, an old German butcher, and a whole lot of drafty old

Victorians. One of those drafty Victorians was left to me in my aunt's will, so Cindy and I moved here from Long Island after my husband, Manny, died.

Getting the house was a bittersweet, survival-level stroke of luck—but a big one, with Manny's benefits tangled up in red tape for over two years. I wouldn't be so scared if it was just me, but I have our daughter to worry about too—to keep warm, sheltered, and fed. I swore on Manny's grave that I'd do my best job. Cindy is the one steady light in my life, and as usual my focus is on her more than anything else as we walk along the sidewalk—up until everything starts going weird around us.

I smell the fresh scent of cut mistletoe first—that slightly astringent smell, mixed with the slightly piney perfume of the berries. I'm used to catching whiffs of it all through the Christmas season, but as I draw near the main street, the wind picks up and blows the overpowering smell of the plant into my face.

I stop, eyes watering from the wind, and look around in confusion. The smell is so intense that it's almost like someone's burning a pile of the stuff. I look around and see no fire, but abruptly notice the sheer quantity of the stuff. Mistletoe is hanging everywhere, all over town.

Every doorway, the corners of every house and awning, the arching light displays running over the streets, the lampposts, everywhere that a sprig of mistletoe can hang, at least one dangles, hung by a red ribbon. I start moving slowly toward the closest one, not entirely sure what I'm seeing.

"Mommy, what's the smelly green stuff?" Cindy is immediately fascinated, but I gently steer her out of grabbing distance of the sprigs. The stuff is poisonous, but the berries smell nice. Bad combination around a tiny kid.

"It's mistletoe, honey. People kiss under it. See?" I point to an elderly couple smooching while a couple of Millennial girls take their picture, looking charmed. The couple is pretty cute. I wonder how many decades of marriage they have under their belt—and then I remember Manny and look away, my heart stinging.

"Oooh. Is it magic?" Cindy sounds excited. Magic is her thing. Her favorite stories are fairy tales—even the creepy ones.

"I don't know," I reply honestly. I'm that way about everything: magic, prayer, Santa, karma, God. I've always believed that any kind of religious opinion or paranormal belief should be sorted out by individuals, and not fed to them by their parents.

I also never want Cindy thinking that I know everything, or that I never make mistakes. No pedestal for me means less chance of disappointing her later—a consideration I wish my parents had given me. Not that I would ever leave my daughter to drag me to bed at night because Mommy and Daddy had too much happy juice, but still.

It's the middle of the day two days before Christmas, and of course the streets are jammed with last-minute shoppers. There's a toy store two blocks down that has plushy snowshoe hares. That's what Cindy wants: a snow bunny. Fifteen dollars plus tax, and enough change left over for a bag of Christmas candy.

Unfortunately, I'll have to push through this gawking crowd to get to our destination. It's not going to be easy—because like me, they're shocked by the sudden appearance of all this ... greenery. And that means they're mostly standing around, blocking my way.

They're either standing around talking about the mistletoe, or bustling around trying to clear it from their properties, sweeping small piles of mistletoe into the gutters—and yes, some of them are standing around kissing under it. It's very cute and kind of ridiculous, and I wonder how many people had to get together early this morning to pull this prank. Not to mention, who they were.

There's a man leaning against a lamppost on the corner as I cross the street. It takes me a moment to recognize him as Jack Whitman, a local billionaire's son and world-class skier. He's beautiful, with his pale face and coal black hair, those bright blue eyes and that deep blue overcoat. He gives me a smile and a wink as I walk past, and I blush slightly while Cindy waves at him.

I wonder what he's doing out watching all this? Is he involved? Is he behind this, maybe? He certainly does seem to be gloating a little. I glance back at him and see that he's wiggling his fingers back at Cindy, his eyes dancing with mischief and good humor. *No way of knowing.*

The Whitmans—just the father and his adult son, as far as I know—live in a giant old house far up the mountainside, and venture down to see us once every week or so. The local rich eccentrics, they are known for their grand gestures around the holidays—such as the massive food donations to the local church that I hope Dr. Whitman will make again. Last time netted each of us enough frozen and canned food to see every poor person in and around Phoenicia through to mid-January.

The elder Whitman is his son's opposite in looks, aside from them both being tall and blue-eyed. Dr. Whitman's complexion is ruddy; his features are generous. He wears a full white beard and mustache, and he always wears a cap over his bald spot, with silver hair flowing from beneath it. Nobody knows why the pair picked a tiny, sleepy town like Phoenicia to settle in, but the kids love them, and they never seem to do any harm.

If the mistletoe prank is their doing, though, this latest grand gesture is ... beyond bizarre.

"I'm cold, Mommy. Can we stop for a cocoa?" The chirpy little voice at my ear drags me back to earth. Cindy's getting big

—I'm strong, but my arm is starting to ache. Still, we only have the one wool blanket to use as a shawl, and I can't wrap it around us both if she walks beside me.

I do a quick bit of poverty math in my mind. A big cup of cocoa with whipped cream and sprinkles for each of us at the candy shop will mean temporary relief from the cold, but no Christmas candy. But I do have baking chocolate, sugar, vanilla, and milk at home.

"Can you hold out until after we get your bunny and go home? If you can wait that long, you can have two mugs of chocolate." Made from scratch, each mug costs maybe forty cents apiece.

I hate having to bargain with my baby daughter over tiny things, but I have no choice. Not even at Christmas. That's just how it is. She'll get two gifts from the toy drive that she won't get to pick, Christmas cookies because I bake them, a five-dollar pizza, one bag of chocolate drops in bright foil for her stocking, and her snow bunny. And then I'll be broke again until my next check, and praying that the Whitmans give us another break.

She lifts her head to peer at me, her dark eyes thoughtful in her round little face. She has her father's looks and his way of drawing her little brows together as she thinks something over. "All right, Mommy," she says very solemnly, and snuggles closer to me. "But hurry up!"

"I'll do my best." The sidewalks are slippery from all the slush from a recent snowfall. The shopkeepers try to sweep the worst of it back into the gutters, but I can feel my worn boot treads slide slightly every few steps. I take deep breaths and fight a surge of panic every time I slip more than half an inch, praying we won't go down in this crowd of shoppers and gawkers.

We're half a block from the toy store when I see a man step out of the tobacco shop two doors down and stop dead for a moment, my eyes widening. It's him—James Norris. Former leading man, billionaire media mogul, and the only man associated with Phoenicia who could give the mysterious Whitmans a run for their money in terms of wealth and success. I've heard before that he sometimes visit town, but I've never seen him myself.

I've had a crush on him since I hit puberty. Now in his forties, he's every bit as hot as he was back when I fell asleep next to open magazines filled with pictures of his tanned and smiling face. His thick brown hair sweeps back from a high forehead; his features are rugged and his mouth generous. His smile is like a flash of light, making his golden-hazel eyes twinkle. Only the slight crow's feet at the corners of his eyes give him away as being over thirty.

He's dressed down today in jeans, snow boots, and a thick Irish sweater in storm-cloud gray. He rocks on his heels as he checks his phone, seemingly oblivious to the gigantic bundle of mistletoe he's just stopped under. We're headed straight for him.

Oh God. For a split second I'm torn between marching up and ambushing him for a kiss that would probably warm me through the next year, and crossing the street just to avoid him. My heart bangs in my ears. I'm suddenly terribly aware of the way my pale blonde hair has slipped loose in wisps from my messy braid, of my cheap lipstick and wind-flushed cheeks.

It's the chance of a lifetime, but weird proliferation of mistletoe or not, I just can't face him.

I take the third option, walking toward him in the crowd, stepping around him politely, and pretending I don't recognize him even though my whole body feels like it's vibrating with rushes of adrenaline. I'm almost past him when I feel Cindy's weight shift. I turn around—just in time to see her lean over and lay a big kiss on James Norris's cheek.

CHAPTER 2

James

I didn't intend to go down the hill to town today. It's ridiculous, really, how I ended up wading through Phoenicia's last-minute shopping crowd while everyone else up at Mom's house had all their presents tucked under the tree already. It's my own fault, though. I managed to leave the Tiffany lamp I bought for my mother's collection sitting on my penthouse couch as I left to drive upstate.

My distraction was understandable; my mother *had* just informed me that Andrea, my ex, would be staying with us for Christmas. The smartest thing that surgically-enhanced little gold digger ever did was ingratiate herself with Mom. I've been looking forward to getting away from my New York City problems for a few weeks. It irritates me to discover that one of the worst of them has followed me home for the holidays.

. . .

MOTHER HAS NEVER FORGIVEN me for breaking up with Andrea, and has tried to get me and Andrea back together more than once. She doesn't understand that Andrea is a high-maintenance gold digger who whines and nags to get her way and refuses to even contemplate having kids. Even if Andrea wasn't a bitch, she's not the one for me, and both she and my mother refuse to see that.

IN A WAY, the errand is a welcome vacation from the tension up the hill. Andrea, demanding that the heat be turned up to eighty, has spent the whole day since I showed up slinking around in a gold lamé mini dress and matching pumps, with her red hair piled artfully and hard gray eyes ringed with kohl. Clouds of musky perfume follow her around; like her artfully revealing taste in clothes, it once attracted me, but now it makes me a little sick.

I CAN'T BREATHE until I go out. Andrea refuses to go out in the cold with me, for which I'm grateful. The only part of me that still likes her is my cock, and the sway of her hips in that tight, shimmering dress had gotten my libido and me into a hell of a fight on the way out the door. It leaves me distracted and thinking of sex—and wishing I had someone kind and friendly to have a little fun with.

Andrea is a particular type of high-end sex worker who doesn't like viewing herself that way. But her brand of trophy wife isn't there to love your kids, or ease away your stress, or do much of anything besides look good on your arm, spend your money, and fuck. Like an escort. Once I realized what she was truly after—and it took me longer than I like to admit—I tried to free myself of her, but she already had her hooks sunk into my family.

DRIVING HELPS CLEAR MY HEAD. Early winter in New York this year was been short on snow until last week, when we got dumped on for four days straight. Now the worst of it is cleaned up enough for people to move around normally, but the whole landscape on either side of the winding mountain road is blanketed in two feet of white.

I PASS by the Whitman's Dutch revival mansion, an enormous white structure with soaring gambrel roofs, a profusion of columns, and trim in scarlet and green. Even during the day those two have enough lights and decorations that their sprawling front lawn looks like a fairy land. The local kids love it; so do I. Andrea, predictably, called it "garish," but she has all the Christmas spirit of a coal hopper.

Phoenicia has gentrified a little over the years, some of the touristy shops giving way to boutiques and specialty stores. One thing it's always been, though, is big on holidays. But when I pull onto the main street and start looking for parking, it looks just a bit like the Phoenicians have gone overboard. What is with all the mistletoe?

I'M STILL WONDERING about that a half an hour later as I step out of the tobacco shop where I've picked up an inlaid wood desk humidor for Mom's new boyfriend, Mitch. It, and the antique jewelry box I got Mom as a substitute gift, nestle in cocoons of tissue paper inside my shopping bag. I've got nothing to actually do back at Mom's place aside from making small talk and dodging Andrea, so I'm trying to come up with excuses to prolong my shopping trip.

My phone goes off as I step outside, and I sigh and reach into my pocket to check it. My mother's number. Of course. Andrea would never call herself, not when she can get my poor, gullible mom to summon me home for her.

Mom means well. She just desperately wants me settled with a houseful of cute grandkids, and Andrea has lied to her about her intentions this whole time. My mom is a very honest woman who has so little experience with lying that she can't tell when she's being led on. So Andrea uses her, and she argues in Andrea's defense in return.

I tuck the phone back into my pocket, determined to at least have a few more minutes to myself. *I'll tell her I was in the shop buying the humidor.* It's the excuse I gave for coming down here, anyway. I'm certainly not admitting to my mother that I left the lamp she's been coveting for months on my damned couch.

Fortunately, her birthday's in January, so she'll just have to wait to get it then.

Phoenicia is lovely as always. I would settle here myself if it wasn't so far from everything I'm doing. As it is, I've thought seriously about weekending over here in a house of my own. But

God, the crowds are thick today. Not that that's any surprise, given the date.

I stand out of the way as best I can, trying to ignore the sharp smell of the mistletoe hanging everywhere. Maybe I can duck into the cafe for some lunch. Or even grab a few more gifts to tuck under the tree. I'm looking up and down the street, weighing my options, when I notice a lovely young mother approaching me.

SHE'S SMALL, youthful, and almost delicate looking, with large, innocent green eyes, wispy blond hair gleaming like spun gold against her pale cheeks, and lips painted a simple pink. I can't see much of her figure under the gray wool blanket she's got wrapped around herself and her child, but that doesn't matter. I'm already charmed. Especially when I notice the lack of a wedding ring.

BEHAVE, I warn myself, though really, the lady's sweet face reminds me of how I've been longing for a little more sweetness in my life. Especially after spending the morning dealing with that bitter, gilded viper that's invaded my mother's home.

THE CHERUB she has with her is dark-haired and olive-skinned, her brown eyes full of wonder at the world as she gazes around. The two of them talk for a moment—and then the mother notices me and hesitates.

I QUICKLY PRETEND NOT to be watching her, busying myself again with my phone. I text my mother with *"in shop, call soon"* and glance up again, noticing the blonde gazing at me all wide-eyed. I've been recognized.

It happens sometimes, even though I've been behind the cameras in various capacities, instead of in front of them, for over ten years. Most people reach a certain level of stardom and wealth and blow it on a lavish lifestyle, drugs, friends, what have you. I invested it, determined to create a production company where I could create good movies without tripping over corporate politics.

Things turned out better than expected. So I've been out of the spotlight for a while, at least on that level. I'm the man behind the curtain now.

But not to this one. I see the old dazzle in her eyes for a moment, and then the most charming attack of shyness that I have ever witnessed. For a moment I wonder if she's going to walk up to me, or run away. I'm disappointed when she lowers her gaze and moves to walk around me instead.

Then the little cherub in her arms, mischief in her eyes, leans over and lays a smooch right on my cheek!

The poor woman freezes, her eyes flying wide open again, and looks up at me in a panic. I let out a laugh, even more charmed than before, and glance up at the bundle of mistletoe hanging directly over my head. "And a merry Christmas to you too," I inform the little girl, who is grinning hugely.

. . .

"Oh my God," the woman mumbles in such a mortified tone that I want to pat her shoulder and tell her it's okay. I mind her personal space, though, and just maintain my smile and shake my head.

"It's no trouble. She caught me fair and square!" I give the woman a smile, and she starts to relax, seeming a little baffled that this is actually happening. *Poor thing. It's all right, dear, I'm not going to bite!*
Unless you want me to, of course.

There was a time in my career when that starry-eyed look coming from a beautiful young woman would have had me angling to get her into bed. With fans, it's generally fairly easy—and fun for all, at least when I do it. Looking at her and at the soft light in her eyes when she gazes up at me, I'm tempted to do it again.

"Yes, I did catch you," the little one insists, and then says firmly, "And that means you owe me and Mommy a cocoa! The kind with the whipped cream and peppermint sticks!" She even pokes a finger into my chest.

The poor woman. It's all I can do not to laugh as she gives her opportunistic child a look of horror. "I—I'm sorry," she starts, but I just smile and shake my head.

"Don't you worry about any of that. I'm charmed, and fortunately for us all, I could really use the distraction." I gaze down at her as she stares up at me, still slightly starry-eyed. Her little girl is beaming with such deep self-satisfaction that I almost start laughing again. This kid really knows what she's doing.

"My name's James," I say warmly, never breaking the woman's gaze. I've missed having someone look up at me like I hung the moon, especially after Andrea's hot-cold mix of manipulative sweetness and disdain. There's nothing manipulative about this woman. "What's yours?"

"Lorena," she murmurs tentatively, as if she's worried I might be playing a prank on her. "This is Cindy."

"Well, pleased to meet you both," I reply, before gesturing toward the cafe. "Now let's all get a hot drink, shall we?"

CHAPTER 3

Lorena

When we walk in the door of the chrome-countered, checker-floored café, I still don't know whether to reprimand Cindy or thank her. Never in my life would I have dreamed that a man like James Norris would end up taking me out for cocoa, but here he is, holding the door for us.

I set Cindy down with a sigh now that we're out of the cold, and roll my throbbing shoulder before removing the blanket and draping it over one arm. She waits beside me patiently, looking around at everything but staying quiet. I take her hand again and we follow the waitress to a table. James pulls out my chair.

As I'm sitting down, my mind's eye suddenly conjures Manny sliding into the seat across from me as I scoot in unassisted. He was young and artless, but devoted—the kind of romantic who had trouble expressing it. He forgot to pull out chairs. I wince slightly, and hide my expression by quickly snatching up a drinks menu.

"Clever of them to sell hot drinks in all these different flavors when it's this cold out," James comments as he sits down. He towers over me, even when sitting—a giant compared to me and Cindy. "I understand that Miss Cindy likes the peppermint cocoa. Do you have a preference?"

He's leaning toward me, his voice a deep, friendly purr, and my heartbeat suddenly pounds in my ears. I can't catch my breath. I can smell his musky cologne, and the faint scent of mistletoe still hanging around him. "I ..." I force out, and then look hurriedly down at the menu.

Maybe I should have just kissed him and been done with it. It can't end up more awkward than this.

"I've never had most of these," I admit finally, in a soft, hesitant voice. If we ever go for a treat, I get a cup of something very plain and let Cindy revel in her whipped cream-covered delight. I've never even *heard* of most of these drinks.

"Well, what appeals?" he asks without missing a beat.

I look down the list and pick one, a little desperate to avoid trying his patience. "Um ... maybe the salted caramel?"

"Salted caramel it is. Clearly you need a treat too, after carrying such a big girl around all by yourself." His eyes dance even more in person than they used to in my magazines. His charisma pulls at me like a magnet. I might have had a crush on him before, but right now, as I bask in the light of his smile, I forget every one of my problems all at once.

How does he do that?

He orders two salted caramel mochas and peppermint hot cocoa, all in their biggest size, and a plate of fruit turnovers to share. Cindy bounces happily at the prospect, and I have to admit my mouth waters a little too. I can bake pastries, but unless I have a lull between my jobs there's no time to do so.

Immediately after the smiling waitress walks away, his phone rings. "Ah, sorry," he says, fishing his phone from his jeans pocket and checking it. He frowns. "It's family. Please give me a moment."

He turns partially away before putting his phone to his ear. "Yes, hi Mom." A pause. His smile starts to look a little forced. "No, I ran into a friend in the tobacco shop, and we're having a hot drink before I drive back up."

I try to distract myself by looking around, but I'm dead curious, and find myself listening in regardless. There's a certain amount of tension to the long pause that follows as his mother talks, as if he's listening to a lecture. "Mom, look, I understand that she invited herself to Christmas, but that is between Andrea and you. She and I haven't had a relationship in several months."

My ears prick up. *What?*

James has been linked for years to the notoriously high-maintenance model-actress Andrea Case. He has never been seen in public with anyone else. But apparently, all of that came to an end earlier this year, while I was too wrapped up in hustling to pay my bills to keep tabs.

"Mom, please don't let Andrea push you around like that. It's bad enough that she invited herself over for Christmas. This is your home, and I came to visit you. Not her. If she can't handle my leaving for a while, she can always come join me."

The corner of his mouth curls knowingly; Andrea doesn't seem the type to brave the snowy streets of Phoenicia, and it seems that he's counting on that.

So Andrea is still following him around even though he's told everyone that they are quits. She apparently is conning his mom and is trying to control him. And he's just trying to come down here for a little break or something, but Andrea won't even allow that. I have a nose for putting stories together, and this one has me intrigued.

"Don't let her worry you, Mom, it's fine. I'll be back soon."

He hangs up and puts his phone away, giving me an apologetic look. "Sorry. Family holiday ... things, you know how it is."

"Not really," I reply honestly, which gets me a sharply curious look. "It's just me and my little one here. My husband died two years ago on deployment."

He blinks in surprise, and his gaze sweeps over us again. I brace myself; he's taking in the thin puffer jackets we're wearing, the wool blanket we were using as a shawl, the careful patch in my shoulder bag. I have nothing to be ashamed of; I'm a good person in bad circumstances, and I'm doing the best I can.

But ... what wealthy man ever sees it that way? Aside from Dr. Whitman and his son, of course. But even they're considered eccentric—exceptions that prove the rule. This man, James, whom I've daydreamed about since I was twelve, has no reason to sympathize. No reason not to dismiss me as cheap, lazy, and just a step above a beggar—if that.

My cheeks burn and my eyes sting alarmingly. My stomach shivers with a mix of humiliation and dread. How will he react?

"Ah, well then. That's unfortunate. I thought perhaps that you were here to see relatives." He seems to want to say more for a moment, but then sits back and smiles at the waitress as she brings our drinks. He seems a little relieved by the interruption.

I'm more than relieved. Though after a moment, I realize that the look on his face is more concerned than anything. I push the conversation on to what I hope is more comfortable territory. "So, you're visiting family?"

I know his mother lives in the area. Every local who follows the movie industry at all knows that. But it seems rude to just assume, as if I know about him from anything besides online gossip articles.

"Oh yes," he says, perking up. "My brothers and I visit my mother every year and stay for a few weeks. She's a bit like the

Whitmans—she goes mad for Christmas and everything to do with it. Her house looks like a parade float right now."

That makes me smile. "That's adorable." My own house, well ... I just can't afford Christmas lights. We have a tiny tree in the front yard that we trim with peanuts and popcorn and let the birds and squirrels eat, only to string up more the next day. But at night, there's nothing in my yard but darkness.

"I'm sorry if I've brought up something that is uncomfortable for you," he says quietly as he slides our drinks to us. They are each in a huge mug, with a small mountain of whipped cream on top. Cindy's has a candy cane stuck into it, which she eagerly pulls out and starts using like a dipping stick. I make sure I have extra napkins handy for her before turning back to him.

"It's not like that. We haven't been on our own very long, and I'm still getting used to Christmases alone." That part's true.

Even back when my parents were too busy drinking to do anything, my Aunt Erin would always take over, making sure that I had something to celebrate, at least for a few days. After she passed away, I had one Christmas with Manny before he shipped out. And now it's been two bleak years of Cindy and I fending for ourselves.

I just wish I could give her a better life than this. Cindy is as happy and content as I can manage. Fortunately she's not a demanding kid. But when she gets older, when she's in school, having a poor single mom will weigh against her socially, just as it weighs against me now.

I don't really have many friends in town. Clients, sure. Nobody has a problem with me doing their books, cleaning their houses, or looking after their pets. They will share a church pew with me, a bus seat, or the counter at the cafe. They just have a problem with being seen with me in any situation where we might be taken for ... peers.

Even now, I can see the curious looks from locals and shoppers as they see the three of us together; the plain, slightly ragged girl, her adorable but inadequately dressed kid, and the billionaire superstar. I know what some of them must be thinking: *what's he doing with her?* And it makes me feel a little better, like I'm thumbing my nose at their stupid prejudice.

Relying on charity upstate, regardless of your run of bad luck, wins you no friends, even when you're a war widow. But James isn't from upstate. And as I notice he's still listening to me and has made no move to leave, I really start to relax.

"Well, that's rather sad. And you live in town, then?" He spoons aside some of his cream to keep it from getting on his nose as he takes a swallow of his drink. "Mm. That's divine. Really, Lorena, you should try this."

I hesitate. It smells decadent enough to make my mouth water, as does the scent of the pastries. I wanted to save it a moment longer, but I need the distraction from the awkward topic.

I scoop up the long spoon and nip up a mix of foam, cream, and caramel drizzle on the end of it. I slide it into my mouth ... suddenly aware of how closely he's watching. I lick the spoon clean, the unbelievable mix of rich sweetness and subtle shifts of flavor melting on my tongue. Then I swallow, taking a little gasp of breath in surprise. "Wow."

His smile widens again. "See?"

"I need help Mommy!" Cindy announces, and I turn at once to help her hold the big mug and avoid getting cream all over her face. She laughs as she gets a little gob on her nose. I hear James chuckling warmly beside us.

I turn back to him and see him looking at us with something I would never have expected. Not pity or amusement, not mockery or barely hidden disdain, but rather ... wistfulness. His eyes are sad, with the warm, longing look of a dog staring after his family's car.

"What is it?" I ask him gently, suddenly too arrested by his unspoken sadness to care much whether I make a bad impression.

"I'm sorry, I just ... your family may be small, but there's real warmth there. That's rarer than it should be." He tilts his head slightly. "So, what do you do for work?"

I squash a moment of defensive nervousness and answer the question directly. "A bit of everything. I've got a client who I'm a personal attendant for, another one I shop for. I take in packages for a dozen people around town and walk several people's dogs. I house sit in the off-season. Things like that."

I wish I could describe my scramble to get enough work in half a dozen fields as something more glamorous, or at least difficult. But the real problem is cramming in enough hours of such work to make ends meet. Rich people don't stay rich by being generous with the help.

His eyebrows rise. "Oh. Well, you know, if you have a card or something, my mother's been looking for a companion. She's in good health, but she doesn't drive, and she spends too much time up on that mountain eating out of cans."

My heart jumps. I don't care that it's not the kind of relationship I wish I could have with the man. It's the possibility of a solid job with a client whose refreshingly non-classist son seems to like me. "I—of course. Just give me a moment."

I'm fishing for a card in the bottom of my bag, wishing I had slipped more into my wallet, when Cindy drops her spoon. "Need more help, Mommy!"

"Just a minute, hun," I say distractedly as I dig. *Of all the times I've carried these cards around and not needed one, now I need one and can't find it.*

"Here, let me help." James quickly moves to offer his own spoon, and Cindy takes it and happily keeps eating the cream off the top of her cocoa.

"Thank you," I say as I finally find one of my simple business cards and hand it over to him. He accepts it, and I settle back to take a swallow of my own drink.

I try to savor it. It's not just a drink—it's a dessert. This and the turnovers are probably the only real treats I'll get this holiday. Soon, though, if this client comes through, I'll be able to afford treats now and again once more.

"So what kind of help would your mother need?" It's an easy topic to jump into.

"Besides driving into town and occasionally going to doctor's appointments, she spends late winter in Florida and will need a sitter for her house and cats. It's not difficult work; she already has a maid. And she loves kids, so you could probably bring the little princess along." He winks at Cindy, who looks back at him solemnly.

I fight down a laugh at my daughter's deepening frown. "Uh oh. Now you've done it."

Cindy folds her arms. "I'm not a princess. I'm a vampire."

"Oh, I'm terribly sorry, my mistake." James puts a hand on his broad chest and I'm all blushes and stifled giggles again, watching. He gives her a confused look. "But if that's so, how can you drink cocoa?"

"Cocoa's yummy. Dracula doesn't drink wine cause he wanted cocoa." She carefully lifts the mug in both hands and takes a wobbly swallow, only spilling a little. I swoop in with a napkin before the droplets can run down her chin.

James is very good with her, I think. At least, from what I've seen so far. He also seems very attentive to my moods and needs, which is rare, especially in a stranger.

Is he putting on an act to impress me for some reason? Or is he sincere, and just better at showing it than many?

I realize that not even Manny was this attentive. Manny, who left a hole in my heart the exact shape of his memory, was a soldier, not a gentleman. Quiet, stoic, who prayed more often than he drank, was shy in bed and yet loving, and spent every minute of his life with me that his military commission allowed.

I loved him. I miss him. But he never had a tenth of the charm of the man across the table from me.

It's been two years and change since I've let a man touch me—since I've even wanted a man to touch me. It's only ever been Manny. Movie-star crushes are just a way of letting off steam.

Until they're in front of you, flesh and blood, friendly and charming as hell, and the possibility of actually going to bed with them becomes a faint blip on the horizon.

Why else would he be so friendly? Is he just horny, or lonely for someone who won't treat him like this Andrea woman seems to? The idea of his being lonely is a slippery slope by itself. It makes my heart open a crack—and with that comes a surge of guilt, because the man I'm feeling that bit of tenderness toward is not my husband.

To this day, I'll never know what secret assignment Manny was on that left him and half his squad dead, with mourning families trapped in the same red-tape nightmare as I. Four of us wives have no bodies to bury, no explanations of what happened. Nothing to show for our loved ones but the government sending empty letters with official words instead of any consideration, financial or otherwise.

How can these men's service not be acknowledged just because the specifics of their mission have to be kept secret? No one has ever had an answer for us. We've been struggling with the help of volunteer attorneys for over eighteen months to get them. But the Veterans Administration has not budged.

The other widows and I still keep in touch. We have an email chain that we share legal information and news on, and chat together. Awkward pen pals scattered across the state, reaching out to each other now and again when the pressure gets to be too much and no one else can understand. It is like having four sisters—sisters in blood.

"I think I could do all of that for her easily. How many hours a day would she need me?" I am praying that his mother will need me a lot. Almost everything else I do can be shuffled around or done on the way to completing other errands. But a solid job where I can bring my daughter? *Where do I sign up?*

"I'll talk to my mother and call you with details," he says brightly as he enters my number into his cellphone. "It won't be more than a day or two."

"Thank you," I murmur, still shocked at the sudden opportunity.

"Oh, don't thank me. I haven't actually had an uninterrupted chat with someone so pleasant since I got here." He winks. "So perhaps I have a few ulterior motives in recommending you."

"O-oh," I murmur, blinking, my heart pounding again. Cindy takes one look at my blushing face and starts giggling.

If you want to continue reading this story, you can get your copy from your favorite vendor by searching for the title:

The Widow's First Kiss

A Billionaire and A Virgin Romance - *Dreams Fulfilled Book 1*

You can also find the e-book version by typing this link in your computer's browser:

https://www.hotandsteamyromance.com/products/the-widow-s-kiss-a-billionaire-and-a-virgin-romance

OTHER BOOKS BY THIS AUTHOR

Saving Her Rescuer: A Billionaire & A Virgin Romance

I was just trying to get away from my crazy ex for the weekend when I ended up in a giant pileup on the highway up to Gore Mountain.

https://geni.us/SavingHerRescuer

Sensual Sounds: A Rockstar Ménage

Lust. Lies. Double lives.

The rock and roll industry is full of people who are looking out for themselves and willing to do anything to rise to the top.

https://www.hotandsteamyromance.com/collections/frontpage/products/sensual-sounds-a-rockstar-menage

On the Run: A Secret Baby Romance

Murder. Lies. Fraud. Just another day in the lives of billionaires and women on the run.

https://www.hotandsteamyromance.com/collections/frontpage/products/on-the-run-a-secret-baby-romance

The Dirty Doctor's Touch: A Billionaire Doctor Romance

I am a master. An elitist. I am at the top of my field, and I know what I am doing.

https://www.hotandsteamyromance.com/collections/frontpage/products/the-dirty-doctor-s-touch-a-billionaire-doctor-romance

~

The Hero She Needs: A Single Daddy Next Door Romance

He's the only man I've ever wanted...

https://www.hotandsteamyromance.com/collections/frontpage/products/the-hero-she-needs-a-single-daddy-next-door-romance

~

You can find all of my books here:

Hot and Steamy Romance

https://www.hotandsteamyromance.com

~

Facebook

facebook.com/HotAndSteamyRomance

©Copyright 2020 by Alizeh Valentine – All Rights Reserved
In no way is it legal to reproduce, duplicate, or transmit any part of this document in either electronic means or in printed format. Recording of this publication is strictly prohibited and any storage of this document is not allowed unless with written permission from the publisher. All rights are reserved.
Respective authors own all copyrights not held by the publisher.

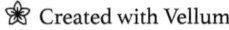 Created with Vellum

www.ingramcontent.com/pod-product-compliance
Lightning Source LLC
LaVergne TN
LVHW011733060526
838200LV00051B/3169